"I DON'T LIKE CHOOSE YOUR OWN ADVENTURE® BOOKS. I *LOVE* THEM!" says Jessica Gordon, age ten. And now kids between the ages of six and nine can choose their own adventures too. Here's what kids have to say about the Skylark Choose Your Own Adventure® books.

"These are my favorite books because you can pick whatever choice you want—and the story is all about you."

—**Katy Alson,** *age 8*

"I love finding out how my story will end."

—**Joss Williams,** *age 9*

"I like all the illustrations!"

—**Savitri Brightfield,** *age 7*

"A six-year-old friend and I have lots of fun making the decisions together."

—**Peggy Marcus** *(adult)*

LOST DOG!

R.A. MONTGOMERY

ILLUSTRATED BY FRANK BOLLE

A BANTAM SKYLARK BOOK®
TORONTO · NEW YORK · LONDON · SYDNEY · AUCKLAND

RL 2, 007–009

LOST DOG!

A Bantam Skylark Book / November 1985

CHOOSE YOUR OWN ADVENTURE® is a registered
trademark of Bantam Books, Inc.

Original conception of Edward Packard.

*Skylark Books is a registered trademark of
Bantam Books, Inc.
Registered in U.S. Patent and
Trademark Office and elsewhere.*

ISBN 0-553-15356-0

Published simultaneously in the United States and Canada

---

*Bantam Books are published by Bantam Books, Inc. Its trade-
mark, consisting of the words "Bantam Books" and the por-
trayal of a rooster, is Registered in U.S. Patent and Trademark
Office and in other countries. Marca Registrada. Bantam
Books, Inc., 666 Fifth Avenue, New York, New York 10103.*

PRINTED IN THE UNITED STATES OF AMERICA

CW   0 9 8 7 6 5 4 3 2 1

LOST DOG!

READ THIS FIRST!!!

This book is about you and your adventures while you look for your dog Ralph.

Do not read this book from the first page through to the last page. Instead, start on page one and read until you come to your first choice. Then turn to the page shown and see what happens.

When you come to the end of a story, you can go back and start again. Every choice leads to a new adventure.

Will you find Ralph? It all depends on the choices you make.

Good luck!

Where's your dog Ralph? **1**

He's not on the porch. He's not behind the garage, either.

"Ralph! Hey, Ralph!" you call. "Where are you?"

There is no answering bark. Ralph had to spend last night outside because he'd chewed up a shoe. (This time it was Dad's shoe.) He must have wandered away!

You run into the living room.

"Dad! Dad! Ralph's lost. He's run away!" you shout.

Your dad lowers the paper he is reading and looks over the top of his glasses.

"You always get too excited," he says. "Ralph is *not* lost. He'll come home."

The paper goes back up.

Next you try your mother.

"Mom, Ralph's gone!"

Your mom is too busy to help.

You try your older brother.

"Beat it, squirt," he says. "I've got important things to do. No time for dogs or little kids. Beat it!"

Turn to page 2.

2   Just then your younger sister, Jessica, comes up to you.

"I'll help," she says. "We could go to the radio station. They report lost dogs and cats."

"Good old Jessica. It's nice to have *someone* I can count on!" you say.

But maybe you should look down by the fort in the woods first. It's one of Ralph's favorite places.

If you go to the local radio station in town, turn to page 7.

If you decide to look down by the fort in the woods, turn to page 8.

"You do it, Jessica," you say.

"Okay. But stand next to me!"

You open the door. You are right in front of a desk. A large blonde woman is sitting behind it.

"Well, what do we have here?" she asks.

You forget all about Jessica and blurt out, "My dog's name is Ralph, and he's lost."

Jessica gives your hand a squeeze. The woman stands up and says, "Right this way. We'll take care of it!"

Turn to page 29.

4   "Okay, Ralph, let Schooner know who's boss!" you say in your loudest voice.

Ralph lets go with a huge bark, followed by an even bigger growl.

You stand your ground. "We mean business, Schooner. Leave us alone!" you say.

Schooner scratches his head and looks at you.

"I'll let you go this time," he says. "But don't come back!"

You, Ralph, and Jessica run out of the woods as fast as you can. You're safe!

The End

"I'm not sure this is going to work," you tell **7** Jessica. "Ralph doesn't listen to the radio, you know."

"I'm not stupid!" Jessica answers. "People will hear 'Pet Parade' and report Ralph if they see him."

The radio station is in a small brick building near your house. You get there in about ten minutes.

"Who's going to do the talking?" you ask. "It was your idea, Jessica."

"Yeah, but Ralph is *your* dog," she replies.

If you insist that Jessica do the talking, turn to page 3.

If you decide to do the talking, turn to page 10.

8   "Ralph loves the fort, Jessica. Follow me," you say.

"I don't know. Those older kids who built it are *mean*!" says Jessica.

"I know, but we've got to find Ralph," you reply.

Soon you come to a clearing in the woods. The fort sits on the edge of the clearing under a large tree. You and Jessica stand behind another tree.

"Quiet, Jessica," you say.

"Why?" she whispers.

"Schooner the bully is there!"

Schooner is talking loudly to two other boys.

"We'll be rich! Rich, I tell you! Hey, what's that noise? Is there anyone out there?"

Schooner stares right at the spot where you're hiding!

If you run for it, turn to page 25.

If you stay where you are and keep quiet, turn to page 14.

10   "Okay, okay, I'll do the talking. But what do I say?" you ask Jessica.

"Just act natural. Just talk to the people the way you talk to me. They don't bite. They don't even bark!" she says, laughing.

"Very funny, Jessica," you answer.

Things go easily, and the radio station helps out. What a relief! The message about Ralph will be broadcast at noon.

You decide not to wait at the station. Instead you'll keep looking for Ralph. You can call the radio station later for messages.

If you check with the police to see if any dogs have been found, turn to page 30.

If you go to look for Ralph at the playground, turn to page 20.

The cabin is very small. There's only room **11** for Old Pete's bed, a desk piled high with books, magazines, and papers, and a small gas stove. Three empty pots sit on the stove.

"Jessica, grab one of those pots and a wooden spoon. Beat on it when I tell you to. We'll scare Schooner and his gang away!"

An hour passes without any sign of Pete, Ralph, or Schooner's gang. Just as you're ready to leave, you see Ralph, then Pete, and finally Schooner and his gang in the clearing.

Go on to the next page.

Ralph takes one look at Schooner. Between his barking and your pot-banging, Schooner and his friends run away.

Pete just laughs. "What a day," he says. "I haven't had so much excitement since the Fourth of July party—fourteen years ago!"

The End

14   "Don't move, Jessica," you whisper. "He doesn't really see us."

"Okay," she whispers back.

Schooner turns away and goes on talking to the others. You catch a few more of his words. He's talking about Old Pete!

Turn to page 18.

You promise Mike Watt that you'll be back **15** after you find Ralph. He says, "Don't let us down, now. You've got a future in radio!"

It's exciting when you imagine having your own kids' program. On the way home that's all you can think of.

"What about Ralph, big shot?" asks Jessica.

That wakes you up from your daydream. She's right. Ralph really is the most important thing. He comes first!

Turn to page 26.

16 Mike Watt takes you into a small sound-proof room and stands next to you. A red sign on the wall blinks "ON THE AIR." You clear your throat and speak into the microphone.

"My dog's name is Ralph, and . . ."

Your message is going out to thousands of people! You feel proud of yourself.

In just a few seconds you're done. You can't believe it was so easy!

Mike Watt says, "Great job. You really do have a perfect radio voice. Hey! How about doing a kids' radio program for us?"

If you tell him that you don't have time to talk about that right now because you're looking for Ralph, turn to page 15.

If you say, "Yes, let's start right away," turn to page 28.

18   Old Pete lives all alone in a little cabin. He's a good friend of yours.

"We'll break into the old guy's house. He hides his money in a big tin can under the floorboards. I've seen him," says Schooner.

"But he's got a dog. I saw it this morning. A big brown-and-black dog," says one of the boys.

"No! That's not his dog. That's just some mutt who comes by looking for handouts now and then. No trouble with him if he's still there."

You turn to Jessica. "It must be Ralph! Ralph likes Old Pete. He visits him a lot."

"What do we do now?" Jessica asks.

If you decide to run to Old Pete's house and warn him, turn to page 23.

If you decide to go home for help, turn to page 47.

"Maybe he wants us to go with him. Probably to help Pete," you say.

"How could he know those bullies are going to rob Pete?" Jessica asks.

"Dogs have ways of knowing things," you answer.

You follow Ralph on the trail to Old Pete's cabin. You get there just in time! Schooner's gang is sneaking up on the cabin. Ralph leaps forward, barking a warning.

Turn to page 34.

20   You and Jessica run toward the playground.

"Ralph loves the playground," Jessica says.

"I only hope he's there!" you say.

But when you arrive at the playground, there is no Ralph. As a matter of fact, there's only one person there—a little kid sitting in the sandbox.

"Boy, is he dirty!" says Jessica.

"Yeah. Wait until his mother sees him," you answer.

"Hey, have you seen a big brown-and-black dog around here?" you ask the boy.

He pours a pail of sand over his head.

"Yup!" he answers. He keeps digging in the sand.

"Well, where is he?" you ask.

"I don't know," the boy says. Suddenly he gets up and runs away.

If you follow him, turn to page 33.

If you let him go and search the playground for Ralph, turn to page 36.

"Schooner and his gang are going to Old Pete's right now. We've got to warn Pete," you say. "I don't think we can make it home and back here with help in time."

Into the woods you go, following a narrow path. It doesn't take long to get to Old Pete's cabin.

But no one's there. No Ralph, no Pete, no nothing!

If you decide to go into the cabin and wait, hoping Pete will come back, turn to page 11.

If you try to make it back to the edge of the woods, where you'll be safe, turn to page 44.

"Run for it, Jessica!" you yell.

Schooner grabs a big stick. He charges after you and Jessica!

"If Ralph were here . . . oh, I wish Ralph were here! He'd save us," Jessica says.

"Yeah," you reply. "Old Ralph would take care of Schooner."

Just at that very moment Ralph appears out of nowhere!

"Ralph! Ralph, where were you?" you shout.

But Schooner is almost on top of you.

If you decide to stay and face Schooner with Ralph's help, turn to page 4.

If you keep on running, turn to page 39.

26 Out of habit, you put your hand down to pat Ralph. He gives you a juicy lick on the fingers.

"Stop that, Ralph! Come on, stop it!" you say.

Then suddenly you realize what's happening.

"Ralph! Ralph! Where in the world did you come from?"

Ralph just looks up and nudges you with his nose. If he could talk, he would probably say, "Aw, come on. You worry too much."

The End

28 Years later, when your children ask you how you became one of the world's most famous radio announcers, you tell them the story of the time Ralph disappeared.

"But what happened to Ralph?" they ask.

"Oh, he showed up. He wasn't lost after all. That's why my program was called 'Ralph's Show.' It was my big breakthrough!"

The End

The woman shows you into an office and **29** introduces you to Mike Watt, the radio deejay. He's the one who reads the news.

You explain the problem.

Mike Watt asks, "How about going on the air? *You* report on Ralph. You've got a good voice."

It's scary, you think. Being on the air will be scary!

Turn to page 16.

30   The police station sounds scary to you. What if Ralph's been hit by a car? But you screw up your courage, and you and Jessica go into the station.

The policeman at the desk looks down at you and smiles. "Well, you didn't rob a bank, did you?" he says.

You explain about Ralph. The policeman says, "I'll check it out right away."

Turn to page 45.

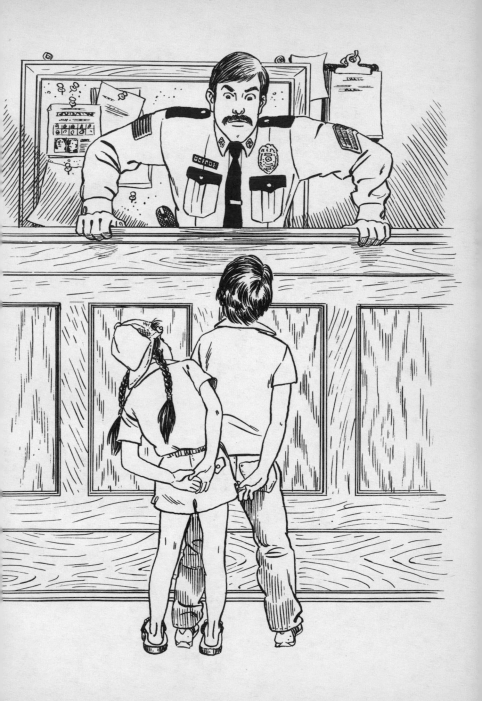

"Come on, Jessica. I'll bet he knows where Ralph is. Follow me!" And you run off after the little boy.

He's fast, but finally you grab him by his dirty shirt.

"Got you!" you say.

"Let me go! Help! Let me go!" he screams. Just at that moment a woman in a floppy hat rushes up.

"Let Henry go at once!" she orders.

"Yes, ma'am." You gulp and let go of Henry. Jessica tries to hide behind you.

"We're just trying to find our dog Ralph," you say.

"Well, this is a *boy*, not a dog." The woman takes Henry by the ear and marches him off.

"What now?" Jessica asks.

"Let's keep on looking," you reply. "We'll find him!"

The End

34   "Let's get out of here!" Schooner yells. He and the other two boys run off into the woods.

Pete comes out of his cabin. "What's all this racket?" he says.

"Schooner and his gang were after your money!" you say.

Pete gives a little laugh. "Well, there is no money," he says. "And what's more, I'm tired of Schooner. This time he's gone too far. I'm going to talk with Schooner's parents tonight!"

The End

"That kid doesn't know what he's talking about. Come on, let's look down by the duck pond," you say to Jessica.

Moments later you are at the edge of a large pond. No Ralph!

Just then another little kid—a girl no more than three or four years old—slips into the pond. Her mother isn't watching!

You jump into the pond.

Turn to page 42.

"Let's get out of here. Come on! Keep **39** going!" you shout.

Schooner and his two friends are right behind you, yelling and screaming. Suddenly Ralph stops short, turns around, and bares his teeth. He gives a low, fierce growl. You and Jessica stop to watch.

Schooner raises his hand.

The fur on Ralph's back rises in a ridge of black and brown bristles. He stands still, growling and barking.

Turn to page 51.

40   You peer underneath the house. It isn't Ralph! It's a little gray-and-black dog.

"Nice dog. We're friendly," you say, reaching down to show her your hand. Jessica backs away so she won't scare the little dog.

Just at that moment, Ralph appears, wagging all over. The dog under the house slowly crawls out. Then you notice her leg. She's hurt!

Turn to page 52.

42   You reach the little girl as fast as you can. She's so scared that she can't scream for help. Her mother sees what's going on and runs into the water. Together you and the mother bring her out of the pond. She's scared—but she's not hurt.

Turn to page 53.

44   Just then you hear a noise. It is a low, eerie sound, sort of like a loon and sort of like . . .

"It sounds like Ralph when he's sick," you shout to Jessica. "It must be Ralph!"

The low moaning sound gets louder.

"Ralph! Ralph!" you shout.

But there is no answer.

Turn to page 40.

The policeman reads the reports on his desk carefully. Then he calls the patrol car to ask if any dogs have been hit. You all hear the patrol car answer over the two-way radio: "No dogs hit by any cars that we know of. No cats either."

"Whew! Wow, I was really worried that Ralph had been hit. Thanks, Officer. We'll keep on looking," you say.

Turn to page 49.

You and Jessica slip away from your hiding place and run as fast as you can toward home.

"What about Ralph?" Jessica yells.

"I don't know," you say. "Let's hurry. We'll have to find Ralph later!"

Just then Ralph dashes out of the woods and runs—thump!—right into you.

"Hey, Ralph! Where did you come from?" you ask.

Ralph gives several low barks and some worried growls.

"What is it, Ralph? What is it, boy?"

Turn to page 19.

"Jessica, we haven't even checked the dog pound yet," you say.

"You're right! Pretty dumb, huh? Let's go," she answers.

An hour later you peer through a fence at a pack of dogs in the pound.

Go on to the next page.

"Ralph! Hey, Ralph! It's us!" you shout.

Ralph leaps at the fence—his tail wagging, tongue licking.

"Okay, Ralph, you'll have to leave your new friends," you say. "Let's go home!"

The End

Schooner backs away slowly.

"I was only kidding. Honest, dog, I wasn't going to hurt these kids! Only kidding. Nice pooch, nice poochy," Schooner says.

Then Ralph gives one giant bark. Schooner and his two friends take off like three rockets back toward the old fort.

"Nice work, Ralph. You saved the day!" you say, giving Ralph a big hug.

The End

52   Ralph nudges the little dog with his nose and whines. Now you understand. Ralph has been trying to help her!

"Good Ralph!" you say. "Jessica, you take this dog back home. Mom will know what to do about her leg. Ralph and I will stay here and scare off Schooner's gang. Right, Ralph?"

He gives a sound that's half-yowl, half-bark. You know he means, "You're right, boss!"

The End

"You're very brave," the little girl's mother says to you. "You saved my daughter's life. Why, without you—I don't even want to think what could have happened!"

She offers to take you home, but you and Jessica say no. "We have to find our dog Ralph. He's lost," you say.

Boy, what a day! You hope it'll end soon— with Ralph found.

The End

ABOUT THE AUTHOR

R.A. Montgomery is an educator and publisher. A graduate of Williams College, he also studied in graduate programs at Yale University and New York University. After serving in a variety of administrative capacities at Williston Academy and Columbia University, he co-founded the Waitsfield Summer School in 1965. Following that, Montgomery helped found a research and development firm specializing in the development of educational programs. He worked for several years as a consultant to the Peace Corps in Washington, D.C., and West Africa. He is now both a writer and a publisher.

ABOUT THE ILLUSTRATOR

Frank Bolle studied at Pratt Institute. He has worked as an illustrator for many national magazines and now creates and draws cartoons for magazines as well. He has also worked in advertising and children's educational materials and has drawn and collaborated on several newspaper comic strips, including *Annie*. A native of Brooklyn Heights, New York, Mr. Bolle now works and lives in Westport, Connecticut.